# Goodnight Me, Goodnight You

For Francesca, Lucian,
Benedict and Derry
T.M.

To my best friend, Russ
M.S.

ORCHARD BOOKS
96 Leonard Street, London EC2A 4XD
Orchard Books Australia
32/45-51 Huntley Street, Alexandria, NSW 2015
First published in Great Britain in 2003
First paperback publication in 2004
ISBN 1 84121 390 X (hardback)
ISBN 1 84362 291 2 (paperback)
Text © Tony Mitton 2003
Illustrations © Mandy Sutcliffe 2003
The right of Tony Mitton to be identified as the author and of Mandy
Sutcliffe to be identified as the illustrator of this work has been asserted
by them in accordance with the Copyright, Designs and Patents Act 1988.
A CIP catalogue record for this book is available from the British Library.
1 2 3 4 5 6 7 8 9 10
Printed in Hong Kong, China

# Goodnight Me, Goodnight You

Written by
Tony Mitton

Illustrated by
Mandy Sutcliffe

ORCHARD BOOKS

Goodnight moon and glimmering stars.
Goodnight swish of passing cars.

Goodnight aeroplane in the sky,
red light, green light, winking high.

Goodnight twinkling lights so pretty
in the distant, glittering city.

Goodnight cows and goodnight sheep
drowsing quietly as we sleep.

Goodnight rabbits hid away
in cosy burrows till the day.

Goodnight bright-eyed birds who rest,

tucked up tightly in their nest.

Goodnight darkness, chill night air,
beyond our window, everywhere.

Goodnight soldiers, tall and still,

who stand like sentries on our sill.

Goodnight den of rugs and chairs,
the place we play at wolves and bears.

Goodnight pirates in their ship,
ready for the next day's trip.

Goodnight picture that we drew:
treasure island, sea of blue.

Goodnight farm upon the floor,
with tractor parked by small barn door.

Goodnight story that we've read.
Goodnight bear beside your head.

Goodnight pillow, soft and deep,
full of peace and dreams and sleep.

Goodnight kiss . . . one cheek, then two.

Goodnight me . . . and goodnight you.